PEEP FOR KEEPS

BOOK SERIES

Published By

OHC Group LLC
PO Box 7839, Westlake Village, CA 91359

TM & © Copyright 2005 by OHC Group LLC. All Rights Reserved.
www.onlyheartsclub.com

SECOND EDITION
ISBN 0-9763213-4-3

Printed and bound in China

The Only Hearts Girls™ formed
The Only Hearts Club® in a bond
of true friendship. They are a fun-
loving bunch of friends who are
always there for one another. They
laugh, share secrets and have the
greatest adventures together. Most
importantly, they encourage one
another to listen to their hearts
and do the right thing.

Contents

Lily's Outdoor Adventure

Lily Rose and her terrier, Cupcake, led the way down the wood-chip-lined path into the woods behind her house. Her teenage sister, Tara, and her friend Taylor Angelique, along with Taylor's beagle, Patches, followed closely behind, taking in the sights and sounds around them. Lily loved the outdoors, and she often invited her friends from the Only Hearts Club, like Taylor, to join her for walks through the preserve. The Only Hearts Club was a fun-loving group of six girls who were always there for one another. They laughed, shared secrets and had the greatest adventures together. Most importantly, they listened to their hearts and always tried to do the right thing, even though it wasn't always easy. Taylor enjoyed these walks, too, since they gave her an opportunity to be close to her favorite things – animals!

The girls had only hiked for a few hundred yards, but they had already seen a bluejay, a robin, lots of

squirrels and even a little bunny. As Lily looked up at the towering trees that lined the trail, her heart soared. There really was nothing she loved more than being outside among the plants and the animals.

"Where are the butterflies you told me about?" Taylor asked.

"Not too much farther," Lily said. "We just have to cross the creek and climb a little hill."

The smell of pine filled the air. It reminded the girls of Christmas, wrapping presents and hanging garlands on the mantle above the fireplace while a warm fire crackled below. The air was so crisp and clean that Lily could clearly detect the scents of wild jasmine and lavender that were just upwind of them.

Their dogs were thrilled to be outside, where they could really stretch their legs. Patches and Cupcake were especially good friends, since they had lived together at Taylor's house for a little while before Taylor gave Cupcake to Lily. The dogs' tails wagged uncontrollably as the wind seemed to bring a million scents to their noses, including interesting ones from bunnies, chipmunks and foxes.

Tara told Lily and Taylor that she was going to stop

here to rest and look at the pretty wildflowers. She reminded the girls to be careful and not go too far away. Lily nodded to her big sister and then raced after her dog.

"Oh, no, Cupcake," Lily said, gently tugging her dog away from a bunny hole she was examining closely. "Your dinner's at home, not in there!" Lily waited for Taylor and Patches to catch up.

"Thanks for taking me on this hike, Lily," said Taylor.

"Sometimes I wish I could live out here," Lily said. "I come here all the time, and you can join me whenever you want." Lily moved easily through the overgrown fern leaves and birch tree branches. Every once in a while, when the brush was really thick, Taylor would lose sight of Lily's long, red hair. But Lily was a good guide and didn't get too far ahead. Soon enough, Taylor would spot Lily's freckled face, looking back and smiling.

Taylor wasn't having quite such an easy time of it. The branches were giving her so many tiny scratching on her cheeks and arms that Taylor felt like the scratching post she kept in her room for her cat,

Spankie. "Maybe someday soon the rest of our Only Hearts Club can come and we can have a picnic in the hills," Lily said, turning to wait for her friend again.

Butterflies and Raindrops

When they reached the creek, Lily pointed out the best place to cross.

"The rocks are slippery," she said, waving her arms for balance as she hopped from rock to rock until she reached the other side. Cupcake bounced easily behind her. Taylor cautiously followed Lily's steps. Patches bounded around her and then…

"Whoa!" Taylor called, and the next thing Lily heard was a loud splash. She whipped around and saw her friend standing in the creek with water up to her knees.

"Oops!" Lily called. "Are you all right?"

Taylor laughed even though she felt a little embarrassed. When Patches barked loudly from the other side of the creek, Taylor thought he was laughing too.

"Yes, I'm fine; just a little clumsy," Taylor said. Lily giggled. She was glad Taylor was OK.

"Come on, then," Lily said, running ahead. Taylor, now wary of the slippery rocks, decided she'd just slosh through the water to the other side. *Why not?* she thought to herself. After all, her pants, socks and shoes were already soaked!

Before long, the girls had reached their goal – the top of the hill. Lily stopped and pointed up. "There they are!"

Above the girls' heads, hundreds of orange-and-black butterflies flitted and fluttered. And what seemed like thousands more clung to the leaves of the trees, which waved in the breeze. The butterflies' colorful wings gleamed in the sunlight. Patches and Cupcake cocked their heads at the strange sight.

"They're beautiful!" Taylor cried. The girls held out their arms, hoping a butterfly would land on them.

"Look!" Lily whispered. A butterfly had landed on her wrist. Its wings opened and closed slowly in time to Lily's breathing. But it didn't fly away.

"I feel one, too," Taylor whispered, but when she looked at her arm there was nothing there. "Oh, wait. It's not a butterfly. It's a rain drop."

Lily looked up into the darkening sky. A cool breeze rustled the leaves. The butterflies flitted closer towards the trees and out of the open air. Suddenly, it seemed, the clouds expanded like wet sponges and merged. A few water drops fell, followed by a steady stream of rain. Since they were too far from home to return without getting soaked, they decided to find shelter and wait out the weather. If they were lucky, it would let up before long.

Taylor found a dry spot under some fallen tree branches and crouched beneath them. Lily and the dogs ran over and crawled in beside her.

"This is turning into an adventure," Taylor said excitedly. Her legs and feet were still damp from her trip through the creek. They were lucky it was a warm day. "Maybe the clouds will open a bit and we'll get a sun shower," she said hopefully.

"And a rainbow!" Lily added. They waited and watched the ever-changing skies.

"Where do you suppose the butterflies go when it rains?" Taylor asked, brushing a strand of her dark

blond hair from her face. "I mean, their wings are so thin and frail. I bet if it rained hard enough, the drops would rip right through them."

"I have a book about butterflies at home," Lily replied. "It says that they huddle together under the tree leaves."

"Just like us," Taylor laughed.

The Baby Bird

Lily gazed out at the falling rain and tried to imagine where all the other animals and creatures were hiding. *Where are the squirrels, the ladybugs and the birds?* she wondered.

"I suppose the animals hide in places like this," she said, looking around the small, cramped space where she crouched with her friend. "The birds must hide under leaves, too," she said thoughtfully, "or huddle in their nests."

"Except for that one," Taylor said, pointing to a spot just beyond their makeshift shelter. A small brown baby bird was lying in the grass near the entrance of their shelter. The bird's soft new feathers were drenched. It was shivering and making small, sad little chirps.

Patches noticed the bird, too. He barked and started moving toward it.

"Patches, *sit!*" ordered Taylor. Patches was well trained, and he sat down next to Cupcake right away.

Crawling slowly and carefully from the shelter, Lily approached the bird, trying not to scare it.

"It's OK, little guy," she whispered in her sweetest, friendliest voice. "I won't hurt you. I promise." She was sure the baby bird would lift its wings and fly away when she got close, but it didn't, which worried Lily immensely. *Maybe it has a broken wing,* she thought. *Oh, please don't!* She was so concerned about the tiny defenseless creature that she didn't even realize how wet she was getting.

"Are you hurt?" she asked it as if expecting the baby bird to answer.

"Does he have a broken leg or something?" asked Taylor as quietly as she could so as not to startle the bird.

The rain was coming down more heavily now. A stream of drops landed on the bird's side, and it let out a startled little peep.

"I think he might be hurt," Lily gasped. Suddenly she was reminded of her old dog, Chip, who had been

ill and had to be put to sleep. The veterinarian had said
that nothing could be done, but Lily hadn't believed
him. She was so sad and angry when Chip had died.
When Lily heard the tiny bird let out a cry, those
feelings came rushing back and she couldn't help
herself. This time she was going to do whatever she
could for an animal that needed help. She hadn't been
able to save Chip, Lily thought, but she *could* help this
little bird!

What Should Lily Do?

Feeling more confident that she was making the bird feel safe, Lily dared to pick up the tiny creature in her hands.

"He looks fine," Lily said, relieved, as she held him up and turned him from side to side, checking for blood or broken feathers. She held him gently against her heart. He flapped his wings weakly and let out a softer peep. She was glad that he seemed to be OK, but she had a funny feeling inside. She knew better than anyone that it wasn't a good idea to touch a wild animal, especially a baby. She tried to ignore the thought. After all, she was trying to help the bird, wasn't she?

"Poor thing," Lily said. "He's just a fledgling."

"A *what?*" Taylor asked.

"A young bird that's just about ready to leave its nest," Lily explained. She felt better about touching the bird now that she could tell he didn't need his mother as much as if he'd just hatched.

"Hey, there's his nest!" Taylor said, looking up and pointing to a low-hanging branch. "Let's put him back."

Lily thought it over. It sounded like a good idea. Just then, something gray flashed past along the ground.

"What was that?" Lily gasped as Cupcake barked madly. Patches didn't seem to notice.

"That was Spankie," Taylor answered, as she managed to hold Cupcake back.

"Who?" asked Lily.

"Spankie, my cat, remember?" Taylor laughed. "He must have followed us out here. Boy, he must not be too happy about this rain. He just *hates* getting wet."

"See, Taylor?" Lily cried. "We can't leave the bird here. I mean, I know Spankie's a nice cat, but he would have gotten this poor little bird for sure if we weren't here!" she shuddered. "Think of all the other wild animals out here that might find our little friend if we leave him. Oh, it's too awful to even imagine!" Lily was convinced that Spankie's brief "visit" was a sign telling her she wasn't just thinking about Chip, but that the baby bird really did need her help.

Taylor read her mind. "Wait, Lily. Think about it. The animal kingdom has survived for millions of years in worse weather than this and with bigger predators than my cat. Let's just put the bird back in his nest."

"We can't just leave him out here all alone!" Lily said with a shudder. "Oh, he's so precious."

"He'll be fine in his nest," argued Taylor. "C'mon Lily, you love nature and you know what's the right thing to do."

But Lily had her mind made up. She looked down at the little bird trembling in her hands. After her experience with Chip, she wasn't going to let anything bad happen to an animal if she could help it. "We need to get him dried and warm," she said to Taylor. "I'm taking him home."

Taylor looked squarely into Lily's eyes. "Only for one night. He belongs here. Can you do that?"

"Sure!" said Lily. Lily was glad that she was

doing something to help the bird, but there was an anxious feeling in her heart. *It is the best thing for the bird, isn't it?* she thought, trying to convince herself.

Going Home

Y ou promise you won't get too attached the little guy?" Taylor asked as she watched Lily rub her cheek against the bird's smooth feathers. Taylor was beginning to wish she hadn't agreed to take the bird.

"Yes," Lily answered and put her hand over her heart. "Only Hearts honor." They both laughed. "Look," Lily said. "The rain's letting up. Let's make a run for it before it starts again." She handed the baby bird to Taylor. "Here, you hold him," Lily told Taylor. "See, I'm not attached." And Lily dashed off as if she really could outrun the weather. Cupcake was once again at her heels.

"Sure," Taylor said sarcastically to herself. She held the bird carefully in her hands as they half-ran, half-slid down the muddy hill. This time it was Lily who lost her balance, but her momentum carried her to the other side of the creek before she had a chance to fall down.

Every few steps Lily turned back to get a peek at the little bird in Taylor's hands. Taylor had tucked him into the cottony folds of her sweatshirt. Patches kept bouncing up around her waist, wanting a look, too!

Lily and Taylor passed a sign that read "Welcome to the Tall Pines Nature Preserve. Hike safely. From this point on, take only pictures, and leave only footprints."

But in all the times she had come to the preserve, Lily had never noticed the second sign just beyond it – until now. The words on this sign were big and dark and red. Lily read them silently to herself:

"REMOVAL OF ANY LIVING THING FROM THE TALL PINES NATURE PRESERVE WILL RESULT IN PROSECUTION TO THE FULLEST EXTENT OF THE LAW."

Lily's stomach was doing flip-flops. By taking the bird home, she was ignoring the rules of the preserve. That just didn't feel right to her. But then she reminded herself why they had taken the bird. *They weren't stealing. They were rescuing. Surely they wouldn't get in trouble for that. Or would they?*

Lily read the new worry on Taylor's face.

"Besides," Lily said as if she had been talking for a while, "there are no signs that say you can't rescue a creature."

Soon they were back at Lily's house. After Lily explained the situation to her mother, her mother said it was OK for Lily to take the bird into the house.

Lily's New Roommate

Lily found an old birdcage from the garage and brought it into her room and put it on her desk near the window. The girls lined the cage with a soft towel and some newspaper, then put in some seeds and fresh water. Taylor placed the little bird inside and turned on Lily's desk lamp so that he would be warm overnight.

Lily looked down at the little bird. He had already fallen fast asleep. Whenever he exhaled, he let out a softly whirring purr, like a kitten. "I think he's going to be fine," she said with a smile. "I also think he likes it here! Let's give him a name. What about Peep? That's what he said when the raindrops hit him!"

Taylor grinned at the cute name, but the stitch of worry she had felt before surfaced again. Naming the bird made him seem like a pet. And they had to take him back to the woods. "Good night, little guy," Taylor said, and she blew a tiny kiss to the bird.

"We'll take you back to the nature preserve tomorrow."
She looked sternly at Lily, who was staring at Peep.
"Right?" Taylor added stringently. Lily didn't answer.
She just placed her hand over her heart and made
cooing sounds to Peep. Taylor sensed that her
concerns about Lily's not wanting to return the bird
to nature were becoming a reality!

After Taylor left, Lily smiled as she peered at the
sleeping baby bird in its cage. Maybe it would be best
for him if Lily kept him as a pet, she thought. Then he
would always be warm and safe and well fed!

But something inside her didn't feel quite right, and
the smile quickly disappeared from her lips. Why did
Lily keep getting these funny feelings?

What's Wrong With Peep?

The next morning, Lily was awakened by a chirping sound. It was Peep! He sure looked better than he did yesterday, thought Lily. His feathers were dry and fluffy, and he was hopping around his cage and singing with a beautiful little voice!

"So you and Taylor will be taking that little bird back to the woods this afternoon after school, right?" Lily's mother asked her at breakfast.

"Um, yeah, I guess...if he's OK," said Lily.

"Well, by the chirping I heard coming from your room this morning, he certainly sounds OK," smiled her father.

Lily just nodded. She didn't really want to think about taking him back just yet.

Taylor came bounding up to Lily that morning at school. "So how's the little guy?!" asked Taylor. "Are

we taking him back to the preserve right after school today?"

Lily shook her head. "Um, he didn't look very good this morning," she fibbed. "I think he's going to need some more time to recover."

"Oh, so he really was hurt!" said Taylor. "We should take him to see my Aunt Tina this afternoon. You know, she's a veterinarian, so she can check him and make sure he's OK."

Lily didn't want to take Peep to see a veterinarian! The vet would say Peep looked fine, and then Lily would have to return him to nature! "You know Taylor, I think Peep is going to be fine. He just needs some time to recover. Last night I looked at a book about birds, and it said that the best thing to do is just keep the bird in a warm place and not move him around too much so he can recover. So I don't think we should take him out of my room just yet to go see a vet."

This explanation sounded a little strange to Taylor, but she had to run to her next class and didn't have much time to talk. Besides, she knew Lily loved nature and would do what was best for the bird.

Lily breathed a sigh of relief. She wouldn't have to take Peep back to the woods today.

When Lily got home, she found Peep hopping around in his cage. But he wasn't singing anymore. "C'mon little guy, let me hear you sing." Lily encouraged him. But Peep didn't seem quite as happy as he had in the morning. Still, Lily loved having the little bird in her room. He was sooooo cute! Maybe she really should keep him as a pet, she thought.

That night, as Lily's mother tucked her in bed, she was surprised to hear chirping. She turned on the light and saw the little bird in the cage on Lily's desk. "Lily?" her mother started, "I thought you were taking the bird back to the woods today. Why is he still here?"

Lily had to think fast. "Oh, Mom, I forgot to tell you," said Lily. "Taylor wanted to be with me when we took Peep back to the woods, and she couldn't come over today after school, so we decided to do it some other time."

"Well, I hope that's soon," said her mother. "I'm sure that bird wants to get back to the preserve, and his mother must be looking for him. I can't imagine how worried I'd be if I didn't know where you were."

"Yes, Mom, I promise," said Lily.

After her mother left the room, Lily started thinking. Was it her imagination, or did Peep seem a little less happy than he had been earlier? Lily thought about her friends from the Only Hearts Club and the pact they had made with each other to try to do the right thing. Was she doing the right thing by not returning Peep to the woods? Lily wasn't sure, but she felt that familiar funny feeling in her heart again – and once again, she ignored it. She liked having Peep around, and he seemed to like being there, she thought as she drifted off to sleep.

Lily Listens to Her Heart

The next morning, Lily awoke expecting to hear Peep singing again. But she heard only silence. Lily jumped out of bed and ran over to his cage to see if he was OK. He was sitting in the corner of his cage, looking out the window, not making a sound. "Peep! Peep! Are you OK?!" Lily asked anxiously. The little bird looked at Lily for a moment and then looked back toward the window. He didn't appear to be sick or hurt, Lily thought, but he did look sort of sad. Peep didn't move or make a sound as Lily got ready for school.

Lily worried about Peep all day. Why was he getting quieter and quieter? Was he sick? Was he hurt? Should she take him to Taylor's Aunt Tina, the veterinarian?

That afternoon, Lily sat near a window at school thinking about Peep again. All of a sudden, a beautiful hummingbird appeared outside the window and hovered for a moment, as if it were looking through the glass at Lily. Soon it was joined by another hummingbird, and the two chased each other around in what looked like a game of tag before they disappeared into the sky.

Lily marveled at how beautiful the little birds looked – so happy and free! Right then, Lily knew what she had to do. She could feel it in her heart. And she had to do it today.

Lily Does the Right Thing

When Lily got home from school, she ran straight up to her room. Peep was still sitting quietly in his cage, looking out the window. He looked at Lily as she entered the room and he flapped his little wings twice.

"OK little guy," Lily said, "let's take you home." She picked up his cage and ran downstairs to the back door.

As she passed through the kitchen, her mother called to her. "Honey, didn't you just get home? What are you doing going out?"

"I'm going to do the right thing, Mom," said Lily. "I'll be back in a few minutes."

Lily and Cupcake walked out to the spot where they had found Peep a few days ago. Lily felt sad about what she was about to do, but she also felt good about

it. She looked inside the cage at Peep, who was looking around.

"Well, Peep, I sure enjoyed having you as a guest," she smiled. "And I'm glad that I was able to help you and make you feel better. But my heart is telling me that you should be free. I know I'll miss you, but this is what's best for you." She opened the door to the cage and gently took out the little towel with Peep still sitting on it. She reached up on her tiptoes and put him gently into the nest in the tree.

Peep looked around for a minute, and then stood on his legs and stretched his wings. After a minute, the little bird flapped his wings and took flight! As Lily watched, he flew high into the air and then landed on a high branch. It was peaceful and quiet, and then Lily heard a familiar sound – Peep was singing!

Lily had a feeling in her heart again, but this feeling was different. She felt good. Peep was back at home, and he was happy. Lily had done the right thing.

Dream Job

When Lily got home, Taylor was waiting for her in the backyard. Taylor looked at the empty birdcage in Lily's hands and said, "I called and your mom told me you were in the woods with Peep."

Lily smiled and nodded.

"I know you might be a little sad, Lily, but believe me, you did the right thing," said Taylor. "You should be proud of yourself for making a difficult decision."

"Yeah, I guess," said Lily. She felt good knowing that Peep was happy, but she also already missed him and felt a little sad.

"Hey Lily," I have someone I want you to meet," said Taylor. "I just asked your mom and she said it was OK."

Lily's mom dropped them off in front of a small white building near Lily's home.

"Where are we?" asked Lily.

"Come on inside and see," said Taylor with a smile.

When they walked through the door, they heard dogs barking, cats meowing and birds chirping. Lily knew where they were right away. They were at Aunt Tina's veterinarian's office!

Dr. Tina came out to greet them. She hugged Taylor and then turned to Lily. "You must be Lily," she said with a big smile. "I'm Aunt Tina."

"Hello," said Lily.

"Taylor called me a little while ago and told me about how you took care of that little bird and how you were going to make a difficult decision to do the right thing and set him free," said Aunt Tina.

"Yeah, I guess," said Lily. "I feel good for him, but I kind of miss him."

"Well," started Aunt Tina. "The reason I asked Taylor to bring you by was that I am looking for someone who has a good heart, loves animals and can help us out here at my office. I can tell from what you did with that bird that you are that sort of person."

"Me? Really?" asked Lily.

"Yes, if you'd like to," said Aunt Tina. "Taylor is going to start helping us next week, and she and I thought it might be fun for the two of you to help out here together!"

Lily smiled. Somewhere not too far away, Peep was probably flying and singing with his family, thanks to Lily's help. And now Lily was going to have a chance to help more animals. She was glad she had listened to her heart and done the right thing.

Read all the Only Hearts Girls' heartwarming storybooks.

It's Hard To Say Good-Bye
When her friend loses her dog, Taylor Angelique finds a new puppy for her. But will Taylor Angelique keep the cute little puppy for herself?

Horse Sense
Olivia Hope's horse develops a slight limp right before the big show. Will she go for the blue ribbon or choose to save her horse?

Dancing Dilemma
Karina Grace is the best dancer in school. Will she let her talent get in the way of her friendships?

Teamwork Works
Briana Joy is a superstar on the soccer field. Will she try to win the game by herself or be a good teammate and help a friend?

Two Smart Cookies
Anna Sophia's pie is ruined just hours before the big bake-off. Can she whip up Grandma's secret recipe in time?

Peep for Keeps
Lily Rose discovers a lost baby bird in the forest. Should she keep it as a pet or return it to nature?